THE DRAGONSITTER Takes Off

THE DRAGONSITTER
Takes Off

Josh Lacey

Illustrated by Garry Parsons

LITTLE, BROWN AND COMPANY
New York • Boston

Little, Brown and Company

Hachette Book Group
1290 Avenue of the Americas, New York, NY 10104
Visit us at lb-kids.com

Little, Brown and Company is a division of Hachette Book Group, Inc.
The Little, Brown name and logo are trademarks of Hachette Book Group, Inc.

The publisher is not responsible for websites (or their content) that are not owned by the publisher.

First U.S. Edition: November 2015
Originally published in Great Britain in 2013 by Andersen Press Limited

Library of Congress Control Number: 2015930245

ISBN 978-0-316-29903-9

10 9 8 7 6 5 4 3 2 1

RRD-C

Printed in the United States of America

THE DRAGONSITTER Takes Off

From: Edward Smith-Pickle

To: Morton Pickle

Date: Monday, October 17

Subject: Bad news

Dear Uncle Morton,

I know you don't want to be disturbed, but I have to tell you some very bad news.

Ziggy has disappeared.

Mom says he was asleep on the carpet when she went to bed, but this morning he was nowhere to be seen.

I'm really sorry, Uncle Morton. We've only been looking after him for one night, and he's run away already.

He must hate being here.

Actually, he did seem depressed when you dropped him off. I bought him a box of malted

1

milks balls as a present, but he didn't eat a single one.

I've been reading your notes. There's lots of useful information about mealtimes and clipping his claws, but nothing about what to do if he disappears.

Should we be searching for him, Uncle Morton? If so, where?

Eddie

Dear Uncle Morton,

We're back from school and Ziggy still isn't here.

While we were walking home, Emily said she saw him having a snack in the café.

I was already running to fetch him when she yelled, "Just kidding!"

I don't know why she thinks she's funny, because she's really not.

Mom called Mr. McDougall. He said he would row to your island first thing tomorrow morning and look for Ziggy. He can't go now because there's a storm.

I'll let you know as soon as we hear from him.

Eddie

Dear Uncle Morton,

Don't worry about my other two e-mails. We have found Ziggy.

He was in the linen closet. I suppose he'd crawled in there because it's nice and warm.

Mom was actually the one who found him. You would have thought she'd be pleased, but, in fact, she was furious. She said she didn't want a dirty dragon messing up her clean sheets. She grabbed him by the nose and tried to pull him out. He didn't like that at all. Luckily, Mom moved fast or he would have burned her hand off.

I think she's going to charge you for repainting

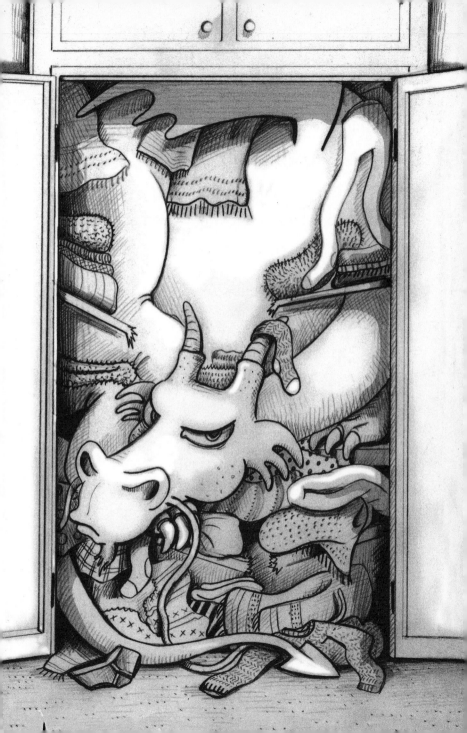

the wall. There's a big brown patch where he scorched the paint.

I still think he might be depressed.

We had mac and cheese for dinner. I saved some for Ziggy and left it outside the linen closet. When I checked just now, he hadn't even touched it.

But at least he's here and not wandering the streets.

Love,

Eddie

From: Edward Smith-Pickle

To: Morton Pickle

Date: Tuesday, October 18

Subject: Ziggy

📎 **Attachments:** Show-and-tell

Dear Uncle Morton,

I just wanted to tell you nothing has changed.

Ziggy won't move from the linen closet.

He still hasn't eaten a thing. Not even one malted
milk ball.

I'm really quite worried about him.

To be honest, I'm also a bit annoyed, because I had been planning to take him to school today.

When I told Miss Brackenbury why I hadn't brought anything for show-and-tell, she just laughed and said I could do it next week instead.

I hope Ziggy will have come out of hiding by then.

Eddie

From: Morton Pickle

To: Edward Smith-Pickle

Date: Wednesday, October 19

Subject: Re: Ziggy

📎 **Attachments:** The yoga retreat

Hi Eddie,

Sorry I haven't replied earlier, but we're forbidden from using any electronic devices at the retreat.

I have sneaked down to the village to read my mail.

Please tell your mother that I'm very sorry about her linens and will, of course, buy her a new set of everything. And don't worry about Ziggy's appetite: If he gets hungry, he will eat.

Thanks again for looking after him. I would never have been able to come here otherwise.

The retreat is exhausting and strangely wonderful. We are woken at five o'clock in the morning and spend four hours sitting in silence before breakfast. The rest of the day is devoted to yoga, pausing only for a meal of vegetable curry and rice. My mind is clear and my body contorts into shapes that would have been impossible only last week.

Love from your affectionate uncle,

Morton

Dear Uncle Morton,

Are you sure Ziggy is a boy?

I think he might be a girl.

I mean, I think *she* might be a girl.

You're probably wondering why I'm thinking this, and the answer is very simple.

She has laid an egg in the linen closet.

Now I understand why she likes being in there. Not only is it nice and warm, but she's built herself a nest from Mom's clean sheets and towels.

The egg is green and shiny and about the size of a bike helmet.

Do you think I could take it to school next week for show-and-tell?

I promise I won't drop it.

Ziggy still isn't eating. Mom says she was ravenous when she was pregnant with me and Emily, but maybe dragons are different.

Eddie

Dear Uncle Morton,

There is a tiny crack in the egg. I'm sure it wasn't there yesterday.

Mom says I have to go to school, but I don't want to. What if the baby comes when I'm not here?

She's calling me. I've got to go.

It's so unfair!

If you get this, please, please, please will you call Mom and tell her someone needs to stay with the egg?

E

Dear Uncle Morton,

I'm glad to say the baby hasn't arrived yet.

When Mom picked us up and brought us home, I went straight upstairs to the linen closet.

The egg was still there.

It has changed, though. It's covered in more cracks.

Also, it keeps shaking and shuddering as if something is stirring under the surface.

I'm not going to sleep tonight.

Eddie

From: Edward Smith–Pickle

To: Morton Pickle

Date: Saturday, October 22

Subject: It's here

📎 **Attachments:** His first step; Birthday boy

Dear Uncle Morton,

This is the most amazing day of my life. I have just watched a baby dragon being born.

I didn't stay up last night. Mom made me and Emily go to bed.

I tried to sneak out of my room, but she heard me and sent me back.

Then I tried to stay awake in my bed, but I must have drifted off, because when I next opened my eyes, it was 6:43 a.m.

I got out of bed and tiptoed down the hallway to the linen closet. I thought I would have missed everything, but there was the egg, still in one piece.

It had changed again, though. It was covered in hundreds of little cracks.

I must have stood there for at least half an hour, watching and waiting, but nothing happened.

I was just about to go downstairs and grab some breakfast when the shell cracked open and a leg popped out.

I stayed absolutely still. I don't think I even breathed.

The little green leg wiggled and waggled. I could see the four miniature claws stretching and flexing as if they were trying to find something to hold on to.

I thought Ziggy might get involved, but she just sat there, watching.

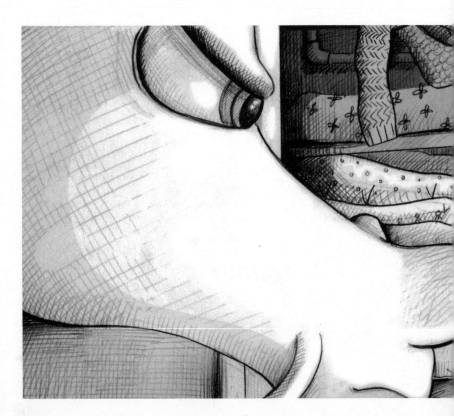

Suddenly, more of the shell shattered and another leg popped out.

Then a bit of a body. And a head.

There it was.

A baby dragon about the size of a small pigeon.

It pulled itself out of the egg and rolled onto the pillowcase, leaving a trail of broken shell.

If I had picked it up (which I didn't), it would have fit in the palm of my hand.

That was when Ziggy finally seemed to notice her baby. She leaned over and started licking it.

I ran downstairs and grabbed some food from the fridge. Ziggy is still refusing to eat, but the baby seems to be hungry. So far, it's had a bowl of milk and eaten two cold potatoes and half a sausage.

I wanted to give it some chocolate as a treat, but I don't know if candy is good for baby dragons.

I wish you were here to see it.

Love,

Eddie

From: Morton Pickle

To: Edward Smith-Pickle

Date: Sunday, October 23

Subject: Re: It's here

Attachments: Beware of the dragon

Hi Eddie,

I was overjoyed to get your e-mail and the beautiful pictures. What wonderful news! I'm delighted, and a little jealous. One of my greatest ambitions has always been to witness the birth of a dragon.

I also feel very stupid. It had never occurred to me that Ziggy might be female. I could have

checked, I suppose, but I know a man who lost three fingers doing that, so I'd never tried.

Which reminds me: Don't touch the baby! It might bite.

I have discussed my circumstances with Swami Ticklemore, and he recommended that I not leave the retreat early. Would you mind taking care of Ziggy and her child for a few more days? I should be able to leave, as planned, at the end of the week.

Morton

From: Edward Smith-Pickle

To: Morton Pickle

Date: Sunday, October 23

Subject: Arthur

📎 **Attachments:** Happy baby

Dear Uncle Morton,

You don't have to worry about the baby biting. He's very friendly and sweet. All he does is play and eat and sleep.

He poops, too, but his messes are very small, so I don't mind cleaning them up.

Emily says he's the cutest thing she's ever seen.

I have named him Arthur. I hope you like the name. If you would prefer something else, please let me know ASAP.

Obviously, I don't actually know if he's a boy or a girl, and I'm not going to try to find out, but he looks very boyish to me.

23

If he ever lays an egg, could you change his name to Gwendoline? That was Emily's choice, and I promised she could have it if he turned out to be a she.

Right now, he is snuggling up with Ziggy in the linen closet. Mom is cooking a big spaghetti bolognese for all of us to have for dinner, dragons included.

Love,

Eddie

From: Edward Smith-Pickle

To: Morton Pickle

Date: Monday, October 24

Subject: Help!

📎 **Attachments:** Him; Mom fights back

Dear Uncle Morton,

You've got to help us. There's a ginormous dragon in our yard, and he won't go away.

He arrived just before bedtime. Mom was running the bath when we heard a terrible bang.

Mom thought the roof had collapsed. I was worried an asteroid had crashed into the house.

We ran outside to have a look.

The first thing we saw was the satellite dish lying in the middle of the yard.

About twenty shingles from the roof had fallen down there, too.

Then we saw why.

An enormous dragon was sitting on our house. Smoke was trickling out of his nostrils, and his tail was flicking from side to side, knocking more shingles off the roof.

Ziggy must have heard the noise, too, because she came outside to see what was going on.

As soon as she saw the dragon, she breathed a huge burst of flames in his direction. I thought it was her way of saying hello, but I soon realized she was telling him to get lost.

It didn't work. The big dragon flew down and charged toward her, gushing flames from his nostrils as if he were planning to roast her alive.

Ziggy sprinted back into the house, pushing Arthur ahead of her.

The big dragon actually tried to follow us inside, but Mom chased him out.

She bashed him on the nose with a broom.

I said she should be careful, but Mom said she wasn't scared of some silly dragon, however fierce he might look.

She just called you seven times. I said you weren't listening to your messages, but she kept leaving them anyway.

If you get this, please call us ASAP.

Eddie

From: Edward Smith-Pickle

To: Morton Pickle

Date: Monday, October 24

Subject: Good-bye????

📎 **Attachments:** I hope he's not hungry

Dear Uncle Morton,

The big dragon is still here. He's lying on the patio, watching us through the windows, as if

he's waiting for the perfect moment to smash through the glass and come inside.

He has scary eyes.

Do you think he could be Arthur's dad? Is that why he's here? Has he come to see his son?

But why won't Ziggy let him?

Can dragons get divorced?

Mom says I have to go to bed now.

If you don't get any more messages from me, it's because I've been eaten by a huge dragon.

Eddie

From: Edward Smith–Pickle

To: Morton Pickle

Date: Tuesday, October 25

Subject: I'm still here

Attachments: Chummy Mummies

Dear Uncle Morton,

We're all still here. Including the other dragon. He spent the night in the yard. There's not much left of Mom's plants.

I think he's been trying to talk to Ziggy. He's certainly been breathing a lot of fire in her direction and making some strange barking noises.

She must be able to hear him, but she pretends not to. She's just been lying in the kitchen with her head in Mom's lap.

I don't know why they're suddenly such good friends.

32

When I asked Mom, she said, "Female solidarity."

I've got to go to school now. I'm taking Arthur for show-and-tell. He's coming with me in a shoebox. I hope Miss Brackenbury likes him.

Love,

Eddie

From: Edward Smith-Pickle

To: Morton Pickle

Date: Tuesday, October 25

Subject: Stuck

📎 **Attachments:** No exit

Dear Uncle Morton,

It's me again.

We couldn't leave the house. The big dragon blocked our way.

Mom told him to step aside, but he refused.

They stared at each other for a long time.

You know how fierce Mom can be, but the dragon didn't even blink.

One of them had to move first, and it turned out to be the dragon.

He breathed a sizzling jet of flame in our direction.

Mom shoved me and Emily back inside, then slammed the front door.

We tried to sneak out twice more, but he was always waiting for us.

So we can't go to school, which is cool.

Maybe this big dragon isn't so bad after all.

Eddie

Dear Uncle Morton,

I was wrong. Staying at home is even worse than going to school. Mom made us do homework all morning. She's going to make us do more this afternoon.

Luckily, I've got an idea for how to get out of here.

I remembered what you said about once taming a big dragon in Outer Mongolia with a backpack full of chocolate.

I'm going to try the same trick with this one.

Wish me luck!

Eddie

Dear Uncle Morton,

It didn't work.

Mom saw me heading for the front door with an armful of candy and confiscated it all.

Now she and Ziggy are sitting on the sofa, watching TV and sharing a box of malted milk balls.

I told Mom she was eating our only chance of escape, but she just laughed.

I think we're going to be stuck in here forever.

Eddie

From: Edward Smith–Pickle

To: Morton Pickle

Date: Wednesday, October 26

Subject: Please call us!

📎 **Attachments:** Mess; Feathers

Dear Uncle Morton,

I know you're not supposed to talk till Friday, but *please* could you call us?

Today is even worse than yesterday.

The dragons have been fighting all morning. The big one broke down the back door and rampaged through the house. He knocked over the TV and broke our kitchen table in half. Also, he knocked almost all the pictures off the wall.

We had to lock ourselves in the bathroom.

We finally came out when the house was quiet.

Ziggy had chased the big dragon into the yard. I don't know how she did it.

She and Arthur are lying on what's left of the sofa. Every single cushion has been burst open. There are feathers everywhere.

Emily is very upset because we've got nowhere to sit.

I'm more worried about what the big dragon will do next.

Mom just called the retreat and spoke to Swami Ticklemore. He said you couldn't be disturbed.

Mom said it was an emergency, but Swami Ticklemore wouldn't change his mind.

If you get this, please call Mom ASAP.

Eddie

Hi Eddie,

I'm very sorry, but I can't leave the retreat early.
Swami Ticklemore says I would do permanent
damage to my inner peace.

I shall hurry out of here at dawn on Friday and come straight to your house.

I don't know exactly why the big dragon is bothering you, but I should imagine he is no different from any other proud father and simply wants to meet his son. Maybe you should let them spend some time together?

If that's not possible, why don't the three of you go and stay in a hotel?

You can tell your mother that I will, of course, pay for the room.

M

Dear Uncle Morton,

Mom didn't like your idea about staying in a hotel.

She looked at me as if I were a complete idiot. Then she spent about fifteen minutes saying why, oh why, was she surrounded by such stupid, selfish men.

I think she means you, Dad, and the dragon.

She might have meant me, too. I'm not sure.

Anyway, Uncle Morton, couldn't you talk to Swami Ticklemore again and ask for special permission to leave early?

Otherwise, you might have to pay for more than one night in a hotel.

If the dragons carry on like this, you'll have to buy us a whole new house.

Eddie

From: Edward Smith-Pickle

To: Morton Pickle

Date: Wednesday, October 26

Subject: Flying

📎 **Attachments:** Up, up, and away!

Dear Uncle Morton,

You won't believe what just happened.

I was in the living room with Arthur and Ziggy when the big dragon appeared at the window. He started breathing fire and making those strange barky noises.

Obviously, I didn't know what he was saying, but I could see Ziggy listening to him. Then she seemed to be talking to him. Finally, she went to the door.

She looked at me. I knew what she wanted. I opened the door. The three of us walked outside—Ziggy first, then Arthur, and finally me.

The big dragon started flapping his wings, slowly at first, then faster and faster.

Arthur hopped onto his back.

They took off.

I thought that would be the last time I would see them. I wished Mom and Emily were there to say good-bye. Then I turned to look at Ziggy and saw she was lowering her neck down to the ground.

There was a strange expression in her eyes.

I realized it was an invitation.

I'm so glad Mom and Emily were upstairs, because if they'd been watching, they would have screamed at me to come back inside.

But I was alone. So I could do what I wanted.

I lifted my leg over Ziggy's neck and climbed onto her back. As soon as I was settled, her

wings flapped and we went up—past the trees
and up above the roofs and up, and up and up
and up and up and up.

I was flying!

I knew I shouldn't look down, but I couldn't stop myself. The yard was already tiny.

I could see the other dragon above us, his huge body silhouetted against the sky.

Higher and higher we went, till we were swallowed by the clouds. I couldn't see anything except whiteness. It was really chilly, too. If Ziggy hadn't been so warm, I would have been frozen solid.

Suddenly, we broke through the top of the clouds, and we were in sunshine. The big dragon was just ahead of us. With a few flaps of her wings, Ziggy was alongside him.

I could see Arthur hopping around on his dad's back, but I held on as tightly as I could, wrapping my arms around Ziggy's neck. I didn't have wings to save me if I slipped off.

Suddenly, the big dragon flipped over. Then right side up again.

Ziggy did it, too.

For a moment I was upside down!

Next, they both looped the loop.

Three times.

It was like being on a roller coaster.

Up and down we went. Around and around. The two dragons took turns doing tricks as if they were saying to each other, *Look at me! Can you do this, too?*

I thought I might be sick, but actually, it was Arthur who was.

I suppose he is only four days old.

The others must have thought he'd had enough then, because suddenly we were diving down, heading for the ground.

We were going so fast, I thought we'd crash through the house. But at the last moment, the two dragons pulled back, and we landed gently on the patio.

The three of them are dozing now, but I wanted to come inside and tell you all about it.

Eddie

Dear Uncle Morton,

Don't worry about leaving the retreat early. You can stay as long as you like. That big dragon has gone, and I don't think he's coming back.

Mom says he probably has another girlfriend somewhere, and maybe he does, but I'm sure that's not really why he left.

I think he came here to see his son, and now he has, so he could go.

Taking Arthur into the air must have been his way of saying good-bye.

I suppose it's the same as Dad taking me to the movies before he drives back to his house.

Everything is very peaceful here, now that it's just the five of us.

Mom and Ziggy are watching a black–and–white movie on TV.

Arthur and Emily are playing Monopoly. Neither of them knows the rules. They're just pushing the pieces around the board and making a mess of the money. Emily keeps giggling, and Arthur is blowing little spurts of smoke through his nostrils.

I hope you enjoy your last day at the retreat, and see you on Friday.

Eddie

From: Morton Pickle

To: Edward Smith-Pickle

Date: Saturday, October 29

Subject: Re: He's gone

Attachments: Home, sweet home; Article

Hi Eddie,

We are finally home after an endless train journey and a stormy ride in Mr. McDougall's boat. The house feels much smaller with two dragons, even if one of them is only a baby. When Arthur grows up, I'll have to build him and Ziggy a home of their own.

I want to thank you again for looking after them so well.

Please tell your mother that I really am very sorry about all the trouble that they caused.

You probably won't like my saying this, but I do think she was right about Arthur. Having a pet is a serious responsibility.

58

If I were you, I would accept her offer. I know gerbils aren't exactly exciting, but you can always get something bigger when you're older.

Will you please also tell your mother that I was entirely serious about the retreat? I could see how stressed she is. Nothing would make her feel better than a week of silence and yoga.

While she is with Swami Ticklemore, you and Emily could stay with me. I know Ziggy and Arthur would love to see you, as would I.

Lots of love from your affectionate uncle,

Morton

P.S. Did you see this?

Saturday, October 29th

The Scotsman

IS IT A BIRD?
IS IT A PLANE?
NO, IT'S A DRAGON!

Photograph courtesy of Annabel Birkinstock

Passengers on a British Airways flight to Paris were treated to an extraordinary spectacle when two enormous green creatures flew past their plane.

Neither the pilot nor the air traffic controllers noticed anything unusual, but at least a hundred passengers are convinced that they were visited by dragons.

Fashion consultant Annabel Birkinstock could hardly believe her eyes. She flies from London

Fashion consultant Annabel Birkinstock

to Paris at least once a month, and has seen everything from David Beckham to the Eiffel Tower, but she was astonished when she looked out the window and spotted a dragon flying past.

"At first, I thought it might be a huge bird," said the shocked twenty-seven-year-old. "But I've never heard of birds breathing smoke from their nostrils."

Aviation expert Graham Tulse has examined photographs taken by passengers on the plane and said the "dragons" were probably just an illusion caused by sunlight and cloud cover.

"One of the passengers even claimed there was a boy riding on a dragon's back!" he scoffed.

Annabel Birkinstock doesn't agree. "I know what I saw," she told us last night. "Those weren't rainbows or shadows. They were undoubtedly dragons."

What's next for Eddie & Ziggy?

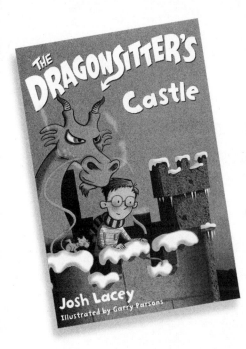

Don't miss their third adventure!

Turn the page for a sneak peek.
COMING SOON

From: Edward Smith-Pickle

To: Morton Pickle

Date: Monday, December 26

Subject: Look who's here

📎 **Attachments:** Unexpected guests

Dear Uncle Morton,

I just tried calling you, but the phone made a funny noise. Have you changed your number?

I wanted to tell you your dragons are here.

They must have arrived in the middle of the night. When I came down for breakfast, Ziggy was sitting on the patio, peering through the window, looking very sorry for herself.

I didn't even see baby Arthur. I thought Ziggy had left him at home. Then I realized he was tucked under her tummy, trying to keep warm.

They're feeling better now that we've given them some toast and let them sit by the radiator.

Have they come to say merry Christmas? Are you coming, too? I'm afraid we didn't get you a present, but there's lots of turkey left and about a million brussels sprouts.

Love,

Eddie

Dear Uncle Morton,

Your dragons are still here. They have eaten the entire contents of the fridge and most of the cans in the cupboard, too.

Arthur also swallowed three spoons and the remote control.

Mom says they will probably come out the other end, but I'm not really looking forward to that.

She wants to know when you are coming to collect the dragons.

We're leaving first thing on Thursday morning, so she asks if you could get here by Wednesday afternoon at the latest.

Eddie

Dear Uncle Morton,

Your phone is still making the same noise. Mom says you've probably been cut off because you haven't paid your bill.

Does that mean you didn't get my e-mails, either?

So, what are we supposed to do with the dragons?

We're leaving first thing tomorrow morning.

Mom has to catch the 9:03 train, or she won't arrive in time for the meet and greet with Swami Ticklemore.

She is going on that yoga retreat like you suggested. She says she deserves it after the year she's had.

I asked if the dragons could stay here without us, but she said no way, José, which you have to admit is fair enough after last time.

Emily and I are going to stay with Dad in his new house. He says it's a castle, but Dad's always saying things like that.

I called him and asked if we could bring the dragons.

He said no, because his new girlfriend, Bronwen, is allergic to fur.

I told him dragons don't have fur, but he said even so.

So please come and get them ASAP.

Eddie

P.S. I've been waiting with my rubber gloves, but there's still no sign of those spoons or the remote control.

Dear Uncle Morton,

Mom says if you're not here in the next ten minutes, she'll leave the dragons in the street and they can take care of themselves.

I said you couldn't possibly get from Scotland to here in ten minutes, and she said worse things happen at sea.

I have literally no idea what she meant.

Now she and Dad are shouting at each other just like they used to when they were still married.

If you get this in the next ten minutes, please call us!

Eddie

Dear Uncle Morton,

I hope you haven't left already to pick up the dragons, because they're not at our house anymore.

Dad said they could come to his castle after all.

I don't know what changed his mind, but he did say the Welsh have always had a soft spot for dragons.

Luckily, Bronwen had stayed behind, so there was room for all five of us in the car.

Dad was worried about his seats, but I told him dragons can be very careful with their claws if they want to, and I'm glad to say they were.

We got a lot of strange looks on the highway, and there was a nasty moment when Arthur flapped his wings and almost got sucked out the window. But we've now arrived at Dad's new castle, and we're all fine.

It really is a castle!

There's a moat and half a drawbridge and a rusty old cannon by the front door.

Dad bought it cheap because the previous owner had lost all his money.

He is going to convert it into apartments and sell them off and finally make his millions.

Our bedroom is in a turret. There's a little wooden staircase that goes to the top, and you can see for miles.

The only problem is it's freezing. Dad says that's the price you have to pay for living in a historical building, but I don't see why he couldn't just buy some heaters.

Here is the address:

Manawydan Castle
Llefelys
Near Llandrindod Wells
Powys, Wales

Dad says please come and pick up the dragons ASAP because he and Bronwen are having a party on New Year's Eve, and they want everything to go perfectly.

Eddie

From: Edward Smith-Pickle

To: Morton Pickle

Date: Thursday, December 29

Subject: Flu

Attachments: Achoo

Dear Uncle Morton,

I forgot to say: Please bring some medicine for Ziggy.

She's got a terrible cold.

When she sneezes, little jets of fire come out of her nostrils. I hope it's not contagious.

Eddie

From: Morton Pickle

To: Edward Smith-Pickle

Date: Thursday, December 29

Subject: Re: Flu

 Attachments: Snow; McDougall to the rescue

Hi Eddie,

I'm very sorry that I haven't replied before, but my communication with the outside world has been severed for more than a week by the thick layer of snow smothering my island. I even had to dig a path from my back door to the shed so I could bring back some dry logs for the fire.

My boat was frozen solid, so I couldn't possibly get to the mainland, and I spent the festive season alone, reading several excellent books and eating my way through whatever I could find at the back of my cupboard. Luckily, I had stocked up during my last trip to France, so I spent

a very happy Christmas eating duck paté and drinking some wonderful red wine.

The dragons weren't so content. They huddled by the fire for the first couple of days, then disappeared. How very sensible of them to come and find you.

I polished off the last of my food last night and raised a red flag. Luckily, Mr. McDougall saw it first thing this morning and came to rescue me in his boat.

I'm now checking my e-mails in his house. He sends season's greetings, by the way, and hopes to meet you soon.

I'm sorry to hear that Ziggy is unwell. Please try to keep her and Arthur comfortable until I arrive. I wouldn't want them to fly any farther south. They'd only get lost.

Mr. McDougall's nephew Gordon is giving me a ride to the train station. I just checked the timetables. If I make my connections at Glasgow and Crewe, I should be with you tonight.

With lots of love from your affectionate uncle,

Morton

THE DRAGONSITTER Series

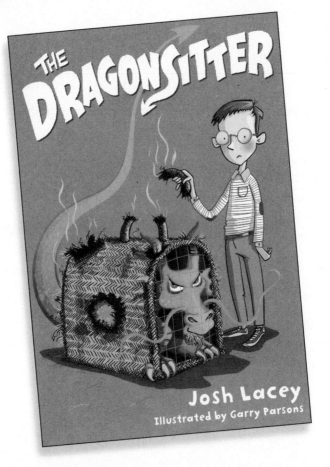

THE DRAGONSITTER

Josh Lacey

Illustrated by Garry Parsons

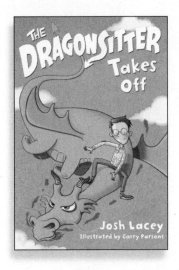

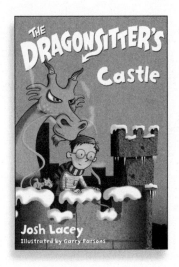

COMING APRIL 2016

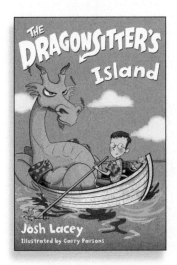

COMING OCTOBER 2016

COLLECT THEM ALL!

If you enjoyed **THE DRAGONSITTER Takes Off**, you might also like these series, available now!

Don't miss a single **SPACE TAXI** adventure!

BOOK 1

BOOK 2

BOOK 3

BOOK 4

Meet
LOLA LEVINE

Second-grader Lola Levine loves writing in her *diario* and playing soccer with her team, the Orange Smoothies. But when a soccer game during recess gets "too competitive," Lola accidentally hurts her classmate Juan Gomez. Now everyone is calling her Mean Lola Levine! What will Lola do?

COMING SOON

About the Author

JOSH LACEY is the author of many books for children, including *The Island of Thieves*, *Bearkeeper*, and the Grk series. He worked as a journalist, a teacher, and a screenwriter before writing his first book, *A Dog Called Grk*. Josh lives in London with his wife and daughters.

About the Illustrator

GARRY PARSONS has illustrated several books for children and is the author and illustrator of *Krong!*, winner of the Perth and Kinross Picture Book Award. Garry lives in London.